Usborne

Build your own
FANTASY
WARRIORS
Sticker Book

Designed by Marc Maynard and Keith Furnival

Written by Simon Tudhope

Illustrated by Gong Studios

Contents

Ravenhold is a land filled with warriors and magic. Many of the most dangerous and powerful warriors are illustrated in this book. Some will help a weary adventurer, and others should be avoided at all costs. Once you've read about a warrior, you can look at the map below to see where they live.

Ramona

Ramona's bow is one of the most feared
weapons in the kingdom of Ravenhold.
Made from the bones of an ancient dragon,
it can strike her target from over a mile away.

STATISTICS

- **Skill:** 9
- **Bravery:** 8
- **Intelligence:** 6
- **Attack power:** 8
- **Realm:** Grimwold Forest

Nagar

They appear like a swarm of bats on the horizon, but the jets of flame give them away – the sky pirates are coming! Nagar leads the raid, his fire sword pointed at the doomed city below.

STATISTICS

- Skill: 7
- Bravery: 8
- Intelligence: 6
- Attack power: 9
- Realm: The Lost Caverns

Molakor

Molakor doesn't need to fight his enemies – not when he has control over time itself! In a blinding flash he turns a young warrior into an ancient pile of bones. Look closely and you'll see his ghost, trapped forever inside Molakor's staff.

STATISTICS

- Skill: 8
- Bravery: 6
- Intelligence: 10
- Attack power: 10
- Realm: The Urghar Wildlands

5

Zanak

Meet the mightiest warrior in the Khaldesh army. The enemies' shields rattle as he steps forward and roars his challenge: "WHICH OF YOU COWARDS DARES FACE ME IN COMBAT?"

STATISTICS

- **Skill:** 7
- **Bravery:** 8
- **Intelligence:** 5
- **Attack power:** 8
- **Realm:** The Khaladz Desert

Griskin

Deep inside his mountain lair, Griskin cackles as he mixes his potions. And today he's concocted a fiendish brew. Smashing it down at the feet of his foes, he turns them all into slugs!

STATISTICS

- **Skill:** 7
- **Bravery:** 3
- **Intelligence:** 8
- **Attack power:** 6
- **Realm:** The Dark Mountains

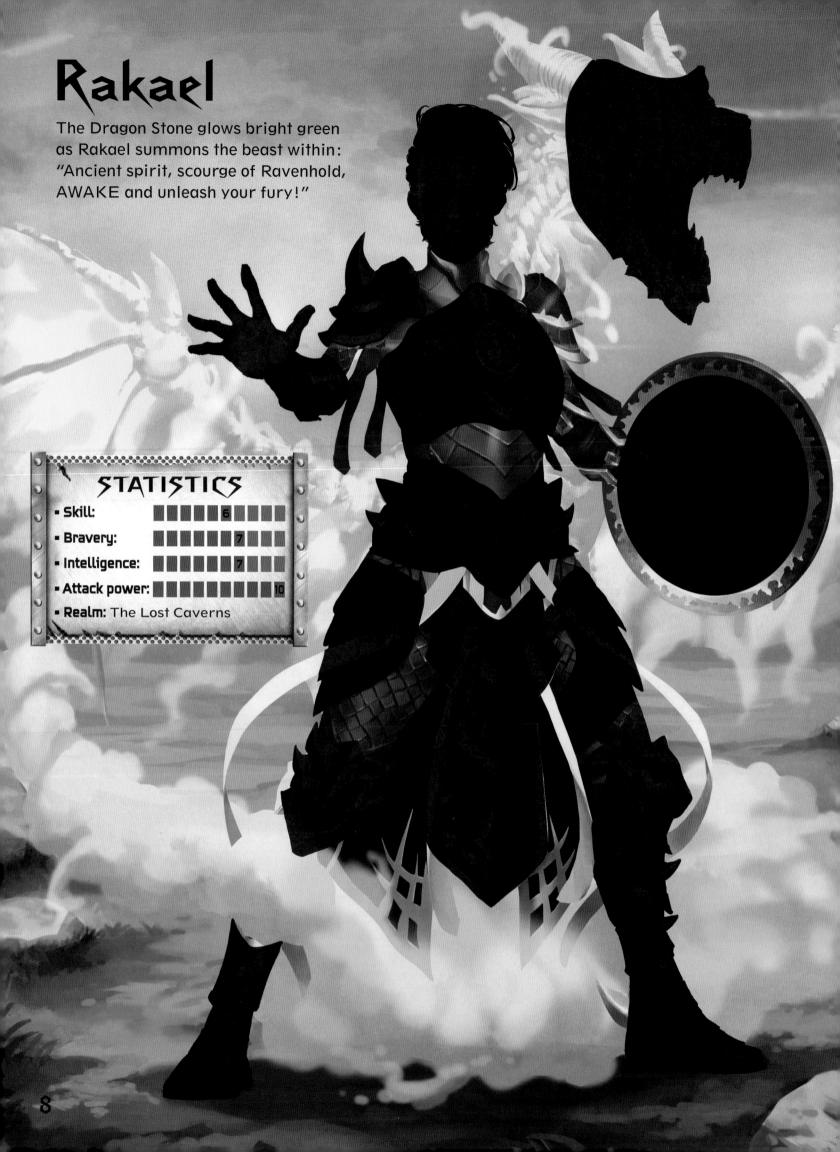

Rakael

The Dragon Stone glows bright green as Rakael summons the beast within: "Ancient spirit, scourge of Ravenhold, AWAKE and unleash your fury!"

STATISTICS

- **Skill:** 6
- **Bravery:** 7
- **Intelligence:** 7
- **Attack power:** 10
- **Realm:** The Lost Caverns

Elador

The city of Stonewall is about to fall. With all hope lost, Elador unsheathes the Sword of Souls. Ancient spells flicker across its blade and reach into the minds of his foes. They drop their weapons and clutch their heads. "Run," the sword whispers. "Run or be cursed forever!"

STATISTICS

- **Skill:** 8
- **Bravery:** 8
- **Intelligence:** 7
- **Attack power:** 10
- **Realm:** Stonewall

Ardana

Storm clouds gather as Ardana takes to the skies. Grabbing bolts of lightning and hurling them to earth, she turns mighty warriors into piles of ash.

STATISTICS

- Skill: 9
- Bravery: 6
- Intelligence: 6
- Attack power: 9
- Realm: Pellanor

Narien

Narien is queen of the Janush – a tribe of warriors who can turn into wolves. She rides into battle on her brother's back, gripping her boomerang blade.

STATISTICS

- **Skill:** 8
- **Bravery:** 9
- **Intelligence:** 8
- **Attack power:** 7
- **Realm:** The Frozen Sea

Karaka

You don't want to anger Karaka – as some bandits are about to discover. They dart in and out like a swarm of flies, but he's surprisingly quick for a man of his size...

STATISTICS

- **Skill:** 7
- **Bravery:** 9
- **Intelligence:** 3
- **Attack power:** 7
- **Realm:** Tanglewood

Aegis

Aegis streaks across the battlefield like a shooting star. Panicked soldiers try to bring her down, but their arrows turn to ashes in mid-flight. With a victorious cry she lets her sun-spear fly... and her target falls in a flash of light.

STATISTICS

- **Skill:** 10
- **Bravery:** 9
- **Intelligence:** 8
- **Attack power:** 7
- **Realm:** The Luru Plains

The Undead

Long ago a rebel army made their last stand on these plains. Every sword marks a grave. As the last man died he uttered a curse: "For a thousand years, when the moon is full, we will rise and take our revenge!"

STATISTICS

- **Skill:** 5
- **Bravery:** 10
- **Intelligence:** 6
- **Attack power:** 6
- **Realm:** The Forlorn Plains

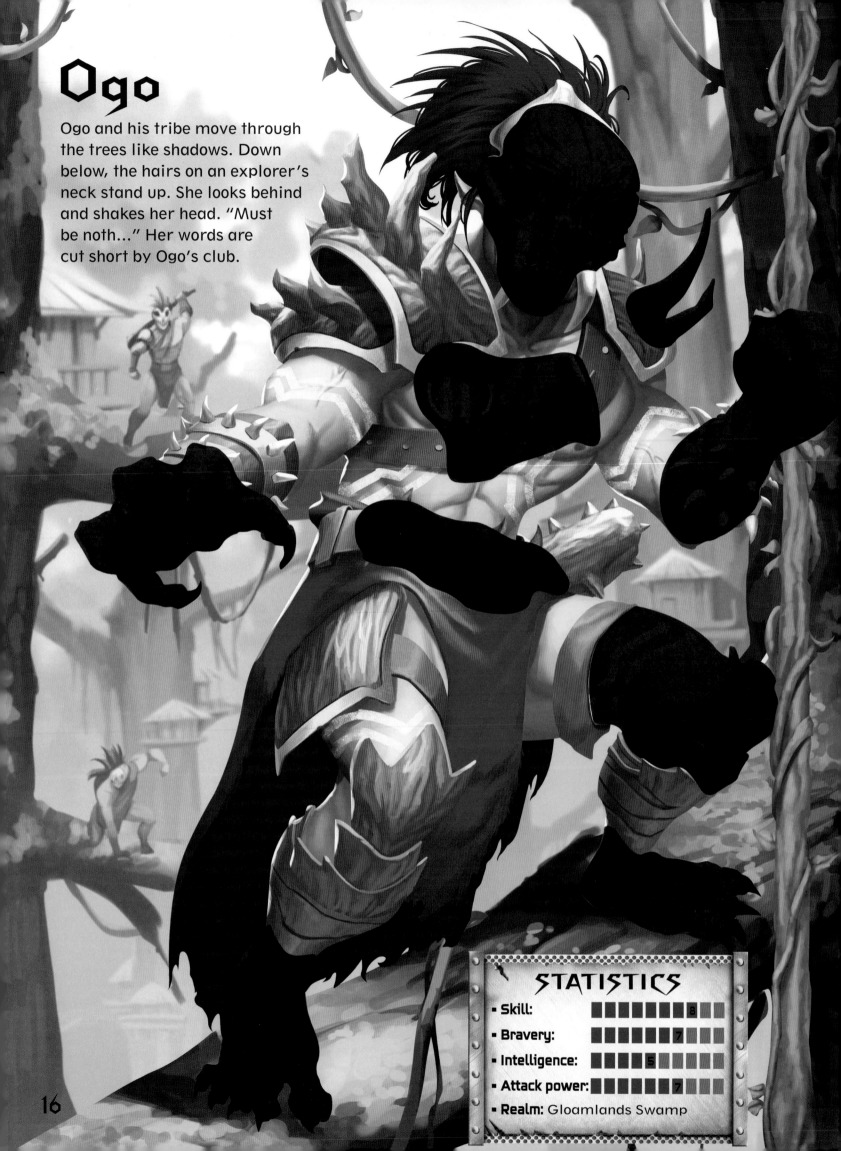

Ogo

Ogo and his tribe move through the trees like shadows. Down below, the hairs on an explorer's neck stand up. She looks behind and shakes her head. "Must be noth…" Her words are cut short by Ogo's club.

STATISTICS

- Skill: 8
- Bravery: 7
- Intelligence: 5
- Attack power: 7
- Realm: Gloamlands Swamp

16

Lokus

The call of his red-eyed raven echoes around the canyon, directing Lokus towards the exhausted fugitive. The chase has gone on for weeks, but now it's over. "Dead or alive?" he snarls. "The choice is yours."

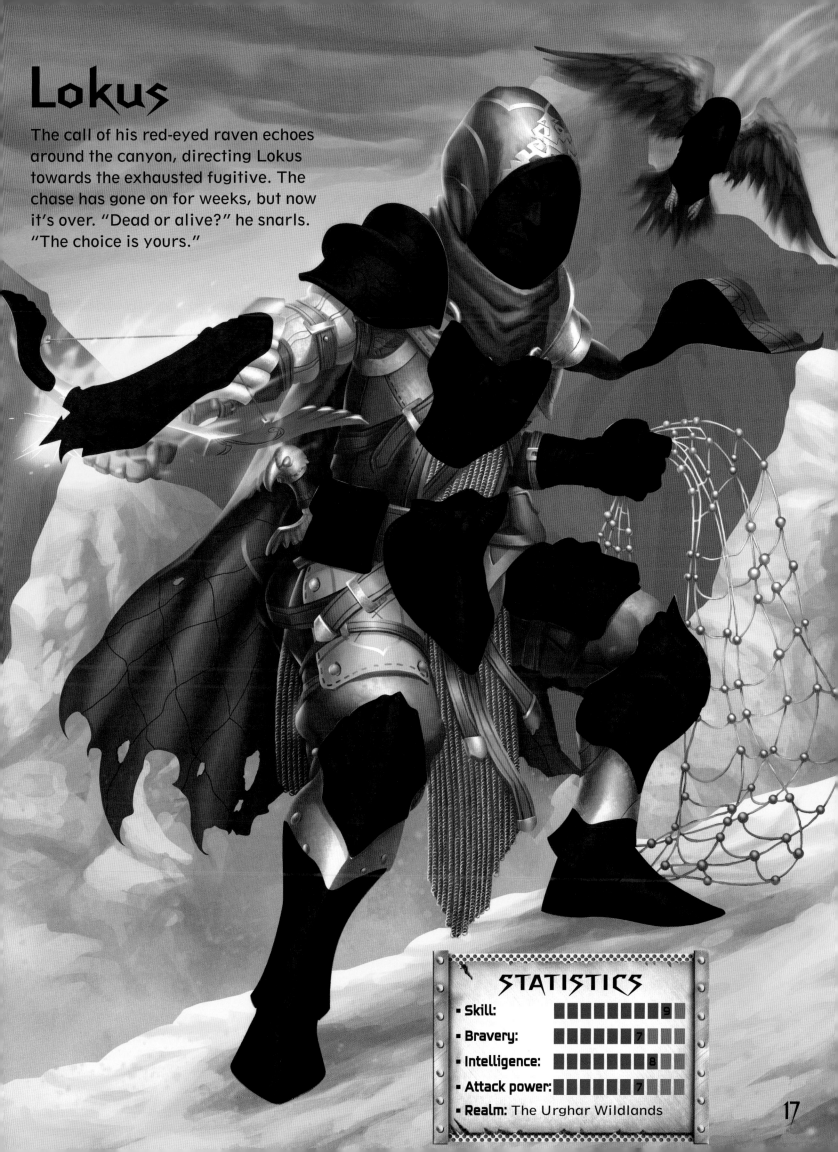

STATISTICS

- Skill: 9
- Bravery: 7
- Intelligence: 8
- Attack power: 7
- Realm: The Urghar Wildlands

Pelaseer

The wind whistles and wails as it whips the sails of an unfortunate ship. But there's something else... A battle cry? Too late the lookout spies the faces in the waves. And then she appears on the tallest crest: the Ocean's Queen... and sailor's doom!

STATISTICS

- **Skill:** 8
- **Bravery:** 8
- **Intelligence:** 7
- **Attack power:** 10
- **Realm:** The Endless Sea

19

Koba

Koba the dragon-slayer waits for her moment to strike. As the beast swoops low, she raises her shield and lashes her tail around its neck. With a deafening screech it crashes to earth.

STATISTICS

- **Skill:** 9
- **Bravery:** 9
- **Intelligence:** 7
- **Attack power:** 7
- **Realm:** The Shifting Sands

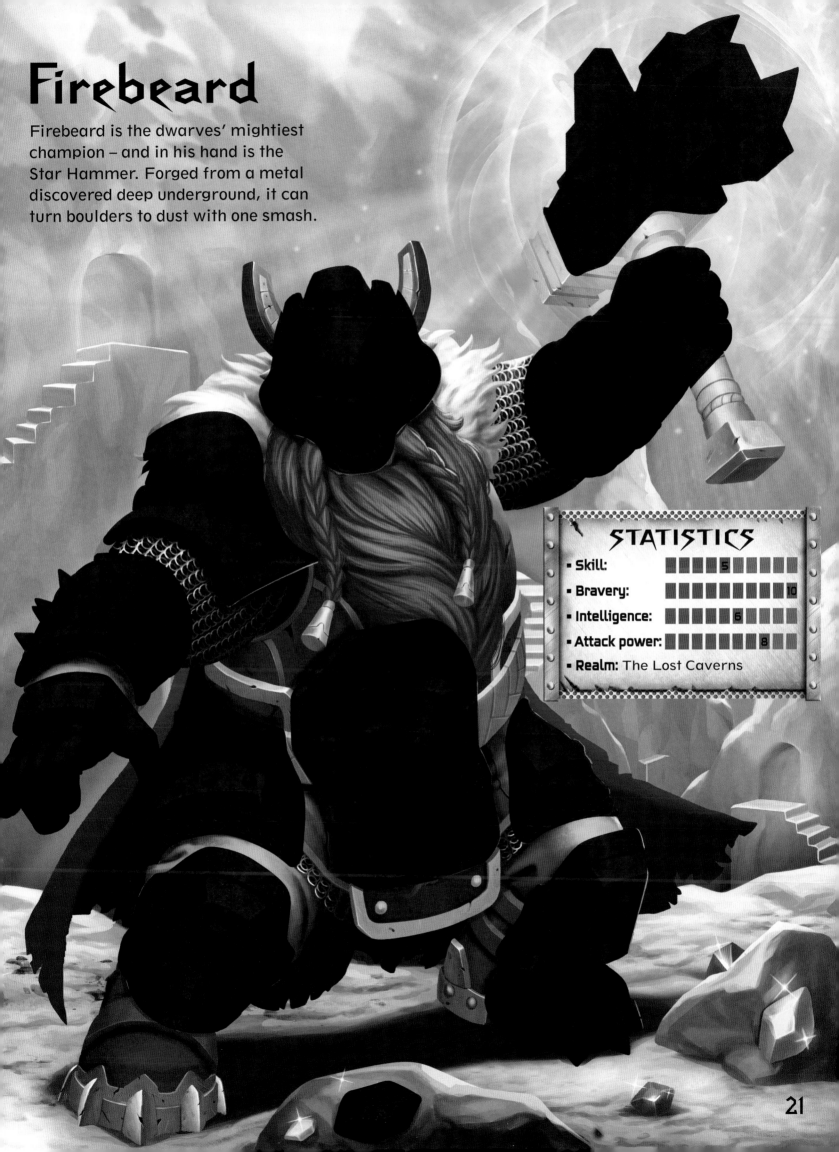

Firebeard

Firebeard is the dwarves' mightiest champion – and in his hand is the Star Hammer. Forged from a metal discovered deep underground, it can turn boulders to dust with one smash.

STATISTICS

- **Skill:** 5
- **Bravery:** 10
- **Intelligence:** 6
- **Attack power:** 8
- **Realm:** The Lost Caverns

Malrug

As an army approaches the city of Pellanor,
Malrug stomps out to meet it. He's an alchemist
who's built a mechanical suit, powered by
mysterious means. "HALT!" he roars.
"You have twenty seconds to surrender!"

STATISTICS

- Skill: 7
- Bravery: 7
- Intelligence: 9
- Attack power: 9
- Realm: Pellanor

23

Glossary

- **alchemist:** a type of scientist who does experiments and tries to transform one substance into another. For example, iron into gold.

- **boomerang:** a thin, curved object that can be thrown so that it spins in a wide arc and returns to the thrower

- **concoct:** create

- **crest:** the top of something. For example, the top of a wave.

- **fiendish:** cruel or nasty

- **foe:** enemy

- **lookout:** a person who keeps watch for danger. On a ship they stand near the top of a mast.

- **rebel:** someone who doesn't follow the orders of their leader

- **scourge:** something that causes suffering

- **shooting star:** a lump of rock, metal and ice that burns as it falls through a planet's atmosphere, making a streak of light in the sky

Edited by Sam Taplin

First published in 2019 by Usborne Publishing Ltd, Usborne House, 83-85 Saffron Hill, London EC1N 8RT, England. www.usborne.com

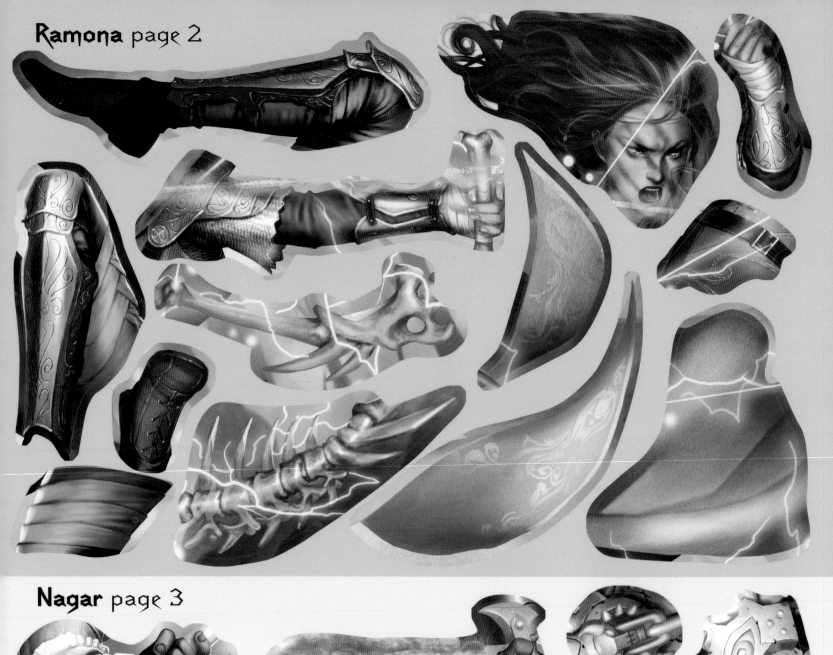

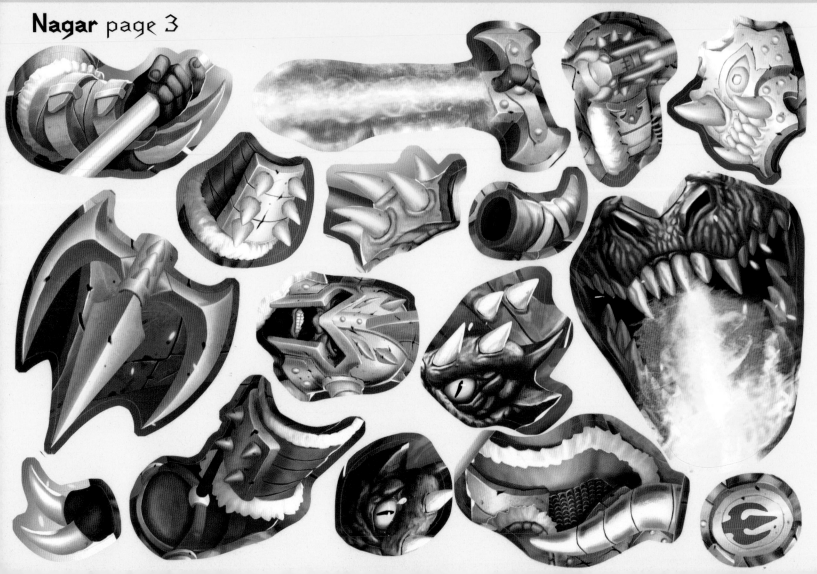

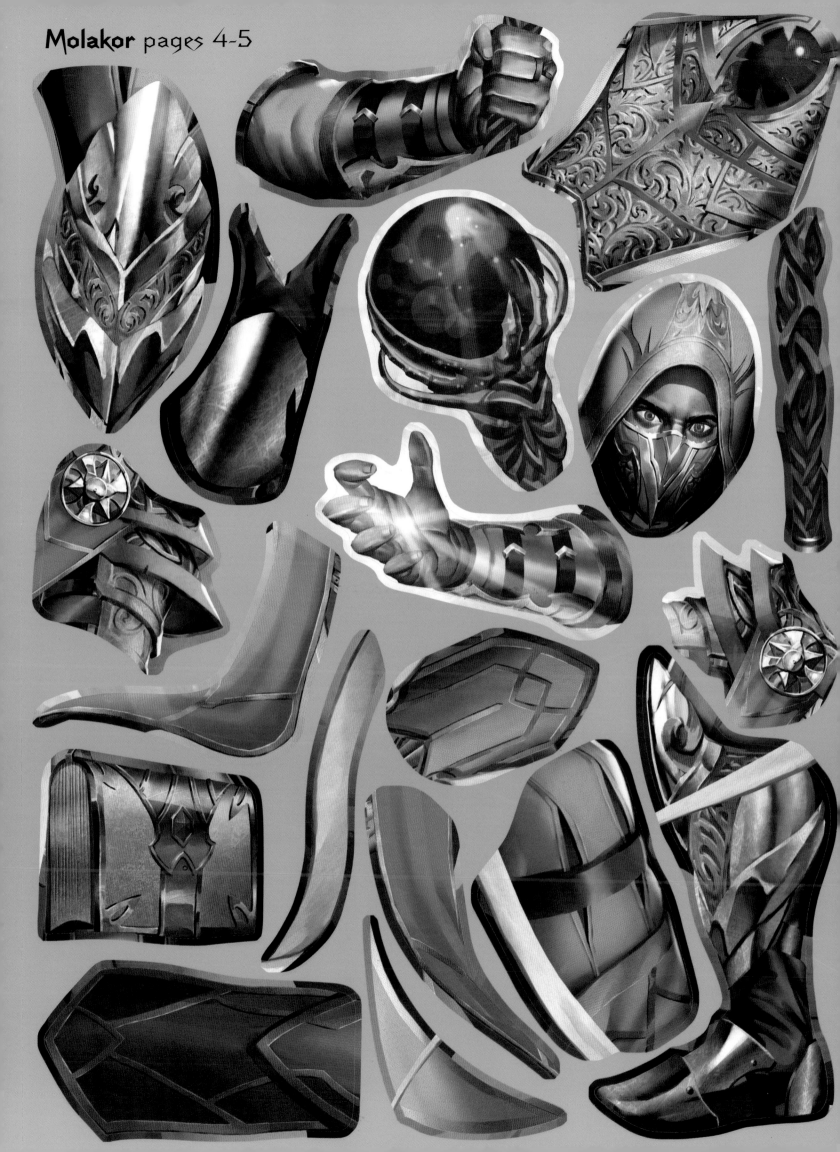

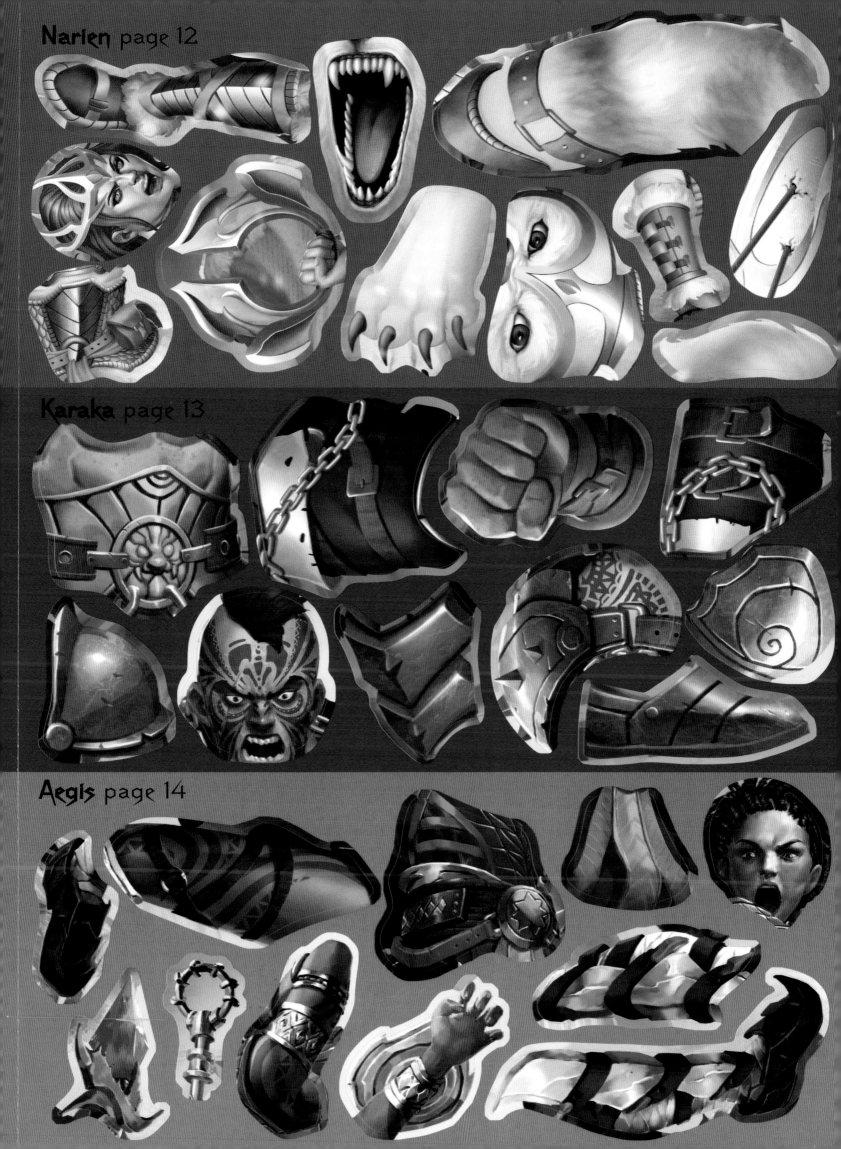

Narien page 12

Karaka page 13

Aegis page 14

Ogo page 16

Lokus page 17

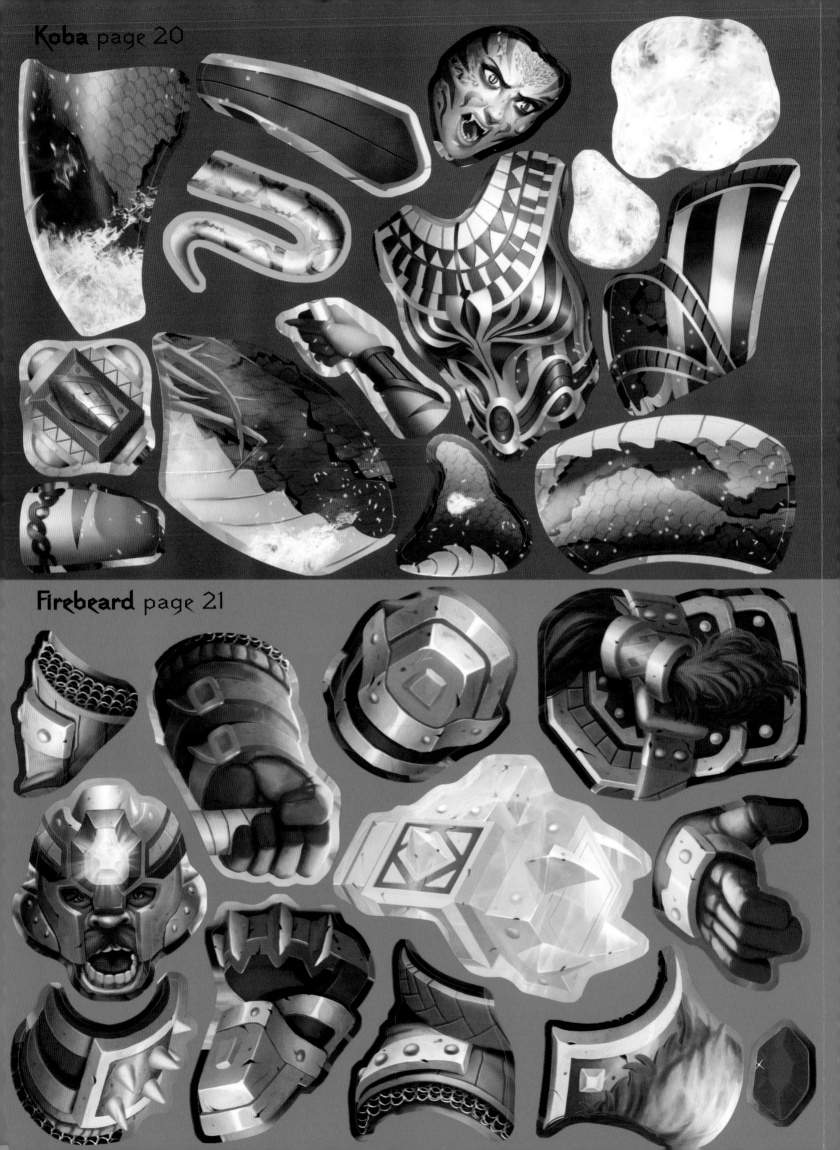